Tonight
is the
Sleepover

by Geoff Patton
illustrated by David Clarke

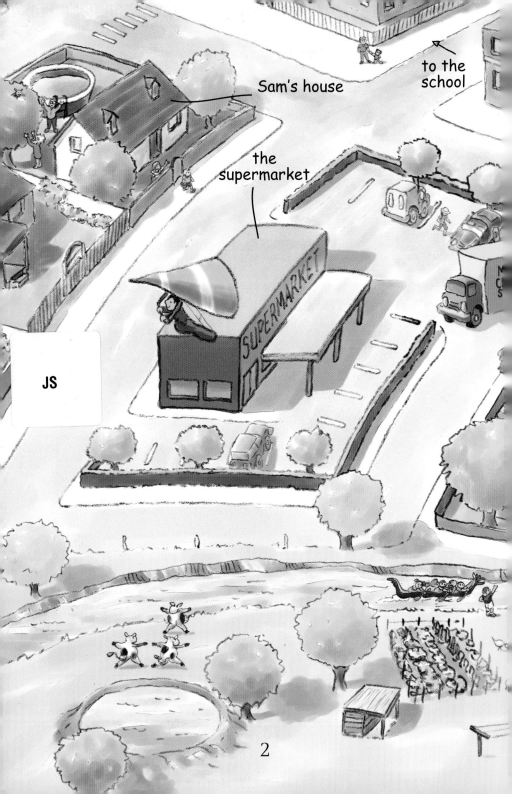

Sam's house

the supermarket

to the school

SUPERMARKET

JS

2

to Emily's house

to Lin's apartment

Con's house

3

Hi. My name is Con
and this is my friend Sam.

Sam

Chapter 1
It's Tonight!

It's tonight! Sam is coming for
a sleepover. I can't wait.
Mum can!
She says that *this* time we have
to do the sleep part
of the sleepover.

I say, 'Mum, the best part of a
sleepover is the staying awake
all night part.'

Mum says maybe there will
be no sleepover after all.

I say, 'I'm only joking.' But I have
my fingers crossed behind my back.
It's hard to go to sleep when you are
having a sleepover.

Chapter 2
Let the Sleepover Begin

Sam is here. He puts on his glow-in-the-dark superhero pyjamas.

'Let's play superheroes,' says Sam. We love to play superheroes.

I zap Sam with my
superhero space beam.
I zap the cat. I zap the wall.
I zap the door ...

... I almost zap my mum.
Oops!
Mum falls on the bed. I say,
'Freeze!'

Mum says, 'Time for bed.'
But it's hard to go to bed
when you are a superhero.

Chapter 3
Shine a Light

We go to bed. I try to sleep. I shut
my eyes. I shut my ears. I even shut
my mouth. But I just can't go to sleep.
I ask Sam, 'Are you awake?'
He doesn't answer.

I shine my torch on his glow-in-the-dark
pyjamas ... by mistake. Now he is awake.
I shine on the cat. I shine on the wall.
I shine on the door ...

... I shine on my mum.
'Oops!'
Go to sleep,' says Mum.

Go to
sleep.

But it's hard to sleep when Sam's
glow-in-the-dark pyjamas are
glowing in the dark.

Chapter 4
Scary Stories

I try to sleep. I shut my eyes.
I shut my ears. I even shut my
mouth. But I just can't go to sleep.
I ask Sam, 'Are you awake?'
He doesn't answer.

I hit him in the leg ... by mistake.
Now he is awake.

We tell stories. Sam tells me a scary story about a horse with no head. The horse has a rider with no head.

I say, 'Sam, if you tell me one more scary story, I will go out of my head.'

'Go to sleep,' says Mum, 'or I will lose my head!'

But it's hard to sleep when I am thinking about a horse with no head.

Chapter 5
Bubbles in Bed

I try to sleep. I shut my eyes.
I shut my ears. I even shut my
mouth. But I just can't go to sleep.
I ask Sam, 'Are you awake?'

I put some gum in his mouth ... by
mistake. Now he is awake.
We chew gum. It's glow-in-the-dark
bubblegum.

Sam blows a big green bubble.
I blow a big red bubble.
Sam says his bubble is bigger
than mine.
BANG!

'Now it's not,' I say.

'Go to sleep,' says Mum.
But it's hard to sleep when
there is bubblegum stuck on
your face.

It's morning. I ask Sam, 'Are you awake?'
The alarm clock goes off ... by mistake.
Now he is awake.

We play superheroes on the bed.

We play superheroes in the hall.

We play superheroes in the kitchen.

'Go to sleep,' says Mum.
'But it's morning!' we yell.

Sam says he had a great sleepover.
I ask Mum if Sam can sleep over
again tonight.

But Mum doesn't answer. I think
she is trying the sleep part of the
sleepover.

Survival Tips

Tips for surviving sleepovers

1 Don't sleep – here's how.

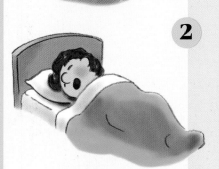

2 Have a big sleep the night before the sleepover. That way on the night of the sleepover you will be able to stay awake all night.

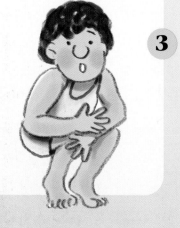

3 Don't forget your pyjamas. It could be embarrassing.

4 Wear glow-in-the-dark pyjamas, they will keep everyone awake.

5 If you want this sleepover not to be your last – don't wake up your mum and dad!

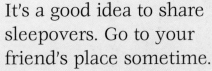

6 It's a good idea to share sleepovers. Go to your friend's place sometime.

Riddles and Jokes

Con My sister thinks she
is a squirrel.
Sam I always thought she was
a nut case.

Sam How do you make a potato puff?
Con Chase it around the garden.

Con What did one ear say to the other?
Sam Between me and you we need
a haircut.

Con Mum, you know how you were
always worried that I would
break your best vase?
Mum Yes, Con.
Con Well, your worries are over.